Sally Noll
THAT BOTHERED KATE

Greenwillow Books, New York

Gouache paints and colored pencils were used for the full-color art.
The text type is Neuzeit.

Printed in Singapore by Tien Wah Press
First Edition   10 9 8 7 6 5 4 3 2 1

Library of Congress Cataloging-in-Publication Data

Noll, Sally.
That bothered Kate / by Sally Noll.
   p.   cm.
   Summary: Kate is bothered by her changing
relationship with her little sister Tory, as first Tory
wants to be with her and copy her all the time and
then Tory neglects her for friends of her own.
  ISBN 0-688-10095-3. ISBN 0-688-10096-1 (lib. bdg.)
  [1. Sisters—Fiction.]   I. Title.
PZ7.N725Th   1991
[E]—dc20   90-38488   CIP   AC

For
Kate Alexis
and Victoria Elizabeth,
with love

Kate's little sister, Tory, was a copycat.
And that bothered Kate.

Everything Kate did, Tory wanted to do, too.

Everything.

"It's part of growing up," her mother would assure her. "She needs you."

But there just wasn't anything Kate did
that Tory didn't want to try.

She wanted to look like Kate.

Once their neighbor
Mrs. Potts said,
"My, you look just like twins,"
even though she knew
they weren't.

And that bothered Kate.

Double peppermint chocolate chip
was Kate's favorite ice cream.
It was Tory's favorite, too.

And that bothered Kate the most.

Then one day Alex asked Tory
to ride with him.

The next week Annie from across the street invited Tory to play.

After that Tory and Annie played often...

and sometimes Tory just wanted to play alone.

It seemed to Kate that Tory hardly noticed her.
And that bothered Kate.

"Is this part of growing up, too?"
Kate asked.

"Yes," said her mother. "I am afraid
this is part of growing up, too."

nore,"

other.
v she needs
e street

As they went down the street, Kate asked, "Tory, what flavor are you going
to have?"
"Double peppermint chocolate chip, of course," said Tory.

And that didn't bother Kate at all.